For Mala, whenever you might find things
too big, too deep, or too scary . . .

Copyright © 2004 by Good Books, Intercourse, PA 17534
International Standard Book Number: 1-56148-447-4

Library of Congress Catalog Card Number: 2004004174

Text and illustrations copyright © Nick Ward 2004

Original edition published in English by Little Tiger Press, an imprint of
Magi Publications, London, England, 2004.
Printed in Singapore

Library of Congress Cataloging-in-Publication Data

Ward, Nick, 1955-
Come on Baby Duck! / by Nick Ward.
p. cm.
Summary: Baby Duck overcomes his hesitancy about swimming when
his teddy falls in the pond.
ISBN 1-56148-447-4 (hardcover)
[1. Swimming--Fiction. 2. Fear--Fiction. 3. Ducks--Fiction.] I. Title.

PZ7.W21554Co 2004
[E]--dc22
2004004174

Come On, Baby Duck!

Nick Ward

Intercourse, PA 17534

800/762-7171

www.goodbks.com

It was a BIG day for Baby Duck.
A VERY big day!
He was going for his first swim
and he was very excited.

"I can't wait," Baby Duck
said to Teddy. "It's going to
be brilliant. The best day ever!"

"Wait for me!" puffed
Baby Duck, waddling
to catch up with his family.
"Hurry up, slowpoke," quacked
his sisters, Minnie and Molly.

"I'm going as fast
as I can. I'm only little!"
"We're nearly there, darling,"
called Mommy Duck.

Splash!

"Look at us," quacked Minnie and Molly.
"Come on, Baby Duck!" said Mommy Duck.
"It's your turn."

Baby Duck stood at the edge of the pond.
"It's very big," he said. "I might get lost."
"Big makes it good for splashing," said Mommy
Duck. "I'll stay close; I love splashing."

Baby Duck looked into the water.
"It looks deep," he said.
"Deep makes it good for diving," smiled
his mommy. "Jump! I'll catch you."

Raindrops started to plop
into the water.
Baby Duck hugged
his teddy.

Splash!
"Jump in, Baby Duck," croaked
Little Green Frog. "It's fun!"
Baby Duck dipped his toe into the water.
"It's cold!" he shivered. His wings
trembled in the wind.

"It's too deep, it's too cold, and . . .

. . . it's scary!"

"My little Baby Duck!" said Mommy.
"There's nothing to be afraid of."
 She gave him a great big hug.
"Let's just watch the fun for a bit."

The rain pattered down and
the wind started to blow.

Splash!

"Dive in," piped the little fish,
leaping out of the pond.
"You can do it!"

"I can't," whimpered Baby Duck,
as the wind blew harder.
"It's splashy and horrible!
I hate it!"

But just then,

who!

The wind blew Baby Duck's
teddy up into the air and . . .

Splash!

"Help!" cried
Baby Duck.
"Teddy can't swim!"

But everyone was too far away. "Hold on, Teddy,"
called Baby Duck. "Here I come!"

Baby Duck jumped.
He dived right in
and he swam
and he swam
and he swam.

"I'm coming, Teddy,
don't worry...

"You're safe now, Teddy!" said Baby Duck. "Well done! You did it!" cried his mommy. "You can swim!"
The sun popped out from behind the clouds. Baby Duck smiled.

"I wasn't scared," said Baby Duck, hugging his teddy. "I love the water . . . and so does Teddy!

"This is the best day ever!"

Splash!